YOU CAN NEVER RUN OUT OF LOVE

For Sally, Clara and Alex; and for Bethan,
who inspired this story – HD

For Carol and Peter Nash – AP

SIMON & SCHUSTER
First published in Great Britain in 2017 by Simon & Schuster UK Ltd, 1st Floor,
222 Gray's Inn Road, London, WC1X 8HB • A CBS Company • Text copyright © 2017
Helen Docherty • Illustrations copyright © 2017 Ali Pye • The right of Helen Docherty
and Ali Pye to be identified as the author and illustrator of this work has been asserted
by them in accordance with the Copyright, Designs and Patents Act, 1988 • All rights
reserved, including the right of reproduction in whole or in part in any form • A CIP
catalogue record for this book is available from the British Library upon request.
978-1-4711-4567-4 (HB) • 978-1-4711-4568-1 (PB) • 978-1-4711-4569-8 (eBook)
Printed in China • 10 9 8 7 6 5 4 3 2 1

YOU CAN NEVER RUN OUT OF LOVE

Helen Docherty and Ali Pye

SIMON & SCHUSTER

London   New York   Sydney   Toronto   New Delhi

You can run out of biscuits . . .

Or run out of bread.

You can run out of energy,

flopped on your bed.

You can run out of chocolates

(none left in this box).

When the washing piles up,

you can run out
of socks.

You can run out of time.

You can run out
of money.

You can run out of patience,

when things don't seem funny. BUT . . .

You can never (no never, not ever),

you can **never**
run out of LOVE.

You can run out of milk.

You can run out of jelly.

If you run out of nappies,

things can get smelly!

You can run out of glue.

You can run out of soap.

When you know it's too late,

THE END

you can run out of hope.

On a very bad day, you can run out of luck . . .

Or run out of ideas,

and get really stuck. BUT . . .

You can never (no never, not ever),

you can never
run out of LOVE.

Love doesn't come
in a bottle or jar.

It's right there inside you,
wherever you are.

You don't have to charge it.
No batteries inside.

Your love can be BIG,
as the whole world is wide.

You can't measure love in a bucket or cup.

You don't have to worry you'll use it all up.

'Cos love's not a game, where you have to keep score.

Whenever you give some,

you'll always have more.

When you've run out of everything else,

you'll still find . . .

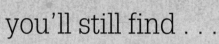

you can **never**
run out of LOVE.